Feathers and Tails

Feathers and Tails

Animal Fables from Around the World
Retold by David Kherdian
Illustrated by Nonny Hogrogian

PHILOMEL BOOKS · NEW YORK

Text copyright © 1992 by David Kherdian
Illustrations copyright © 1992 by Nonny H. Kherdian
Published by Philomel Books, a division of The Putnam & Grosset Group,
200 Madison Avenue, New York, NY 10016.
All rights reserved. Published simultaneously in Canada.
Printed in Mexico.
Book design by Nonny Hogrogian
Lettering by David Gatti
Library of Congress Cataloging-in-Publication Data
Kherdian, David.   Feathers and tails / retold by David Kherdian;
illustrated by Nonny Hogrogian.   p.   cm.
Summary: A collection of animal fables and folklore from such sources
as the Bidpai fables, Aesop, Panchatantra, Grimm, and Wu Cheng-en
ISBN 0-399-21876-9
1. Fables. 2. Tales. [1. Fables. 2. Animals—Folklore.]
I. Hogrogian, Nonny, ill.   II. Title.
PZ8.2.K47Fe 1992 398.2 [E]—dc20 91-31270 CIP AC
1 3 5 7 9 10 8 6 4 2
First Impression

To Patti

Contents

Introduction

Legends, fables, folktales, and proverbs constitute the oldest forms of storytelling. Firmly grounded in moral tradition, they were handed down from generation to generation. The purpose of this tradition was to preserve a people's lore and truth in a form that could be communicated to succeeding generations, to demonstrate not only what had been accumulated and understood about life and living, but to help others on the long path of life that is filled with pitfalls and dangers at every turn.

These stories have reached us from all the peoples of the Earth, and in a variety of forms. But they are almost certainly drawn from a single source, the Bidpai Fables, which came from the East, were carried to Persia, and later forwarded to Greece and the rest of the world.

These stories speak to our limitations as well as our possibilities, since one without the other is meaningless. We are confused by our potential, our possibilities. Each of us is born knowing there is more—but more of what? As we grow and begin to define what the more is for ourselves, we see that it is nothing more or less than our own wholeness. We need guidance, but we are uncertain how to seek it, or how to apply it once it has been found. In all of this the ancient teaching story can be our guide, for it speaks to us with humor, laughter, and enjoyment, from a source that we can all recognize because it is as old as mankind, as universal as the sun and stars.

The animal fable is perhaps the most endearing of this ancient form because it is the most indirect. We can bear very little direct instruction. We are understandably sensitive about our weaknesses because we know how difficult they are to overcome. For this reason we are blind to many of our faults and have great difficulty seeing ourselves as others see us. But we can see in the animal traits of these stories aspects of the human—not only the foibles and follies of others, but our own shortcomings as well. And in seeing this we are linked with others. In seeing this we share in our common humanity, for we are all brothers under the skin.

D. K.

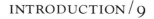

The Four Friends

It was in another time, long, long ago, that a wise old crow lived in a ginkgo tree. From his favorite perch he could look out over all of the land that he had come to think of as his own. Although he had many friends in the forests and valleys—foxes, tigers, bears, and badgers, to name just a few—he liked to keep to himself most of the time.

One day, while Crow was sitting on his favorite branch high up in the ginkgo tree that was his home, a hunter came and spread a large net beneath his perch. He sprinkled it with fine, yellow seeds. Crow never stirred but sat and watched as the hunter disappeared into the brush. It wasn't long before a flock of doves gathered on the ground and without noticing the net began pecking at the seeds.

Crow was about to holler down to warn them when one of the doves stepped on the drawstring, and WHOOSH, the net suddenly drew up around their bodies and trapped them inside. The doves began squirming and crying, but their leader called out, "Flap your wings, flap your wings!" He knew that the hunter would soon be returning for his catch and if they didn't get away at once, they would all be killed. The doves began flapping their wings for all they were worth, and an amazing thing happened: the net began slowly to rise into the air.

Crow was amazed, not only by the cleverness of the leader, but by the sight of the flying net!

Crow flew straight up from his perch and began flapping his own wings in imitation to encourage them. He was cheering for the doves to escape. The doves rose higher and higher, clearing the trees at the edge of the wood. Crow flew behind them and above them and around them, even ahead of them, cawing as loud as he could.

The doves flew on and on, until at last they dropped from exhaustion, tumbling in a heap upon the ground. And there they lay, one on top of another, too weak to move.

Crow flew to a nearby tree and stared down at the trapped doves who were trying to flap and flutter as best they could. They had escaped their clever captor, but they were still held fast inside their knotty prison.

Just then Crow spotted a mouse peering out from his burrow in the meadow. Mouse sniffed the air and stared all around. He raced over to the doves who were chirping feebly to one another. Without a moment's hesitation, Mouse began chewing on the ropes. He chewed and chewed until he had made a small opening.

Crow looked down in amazement as the doves began popping out of the net, one by one. Flying up and down, the doves began chirping and cooing and congratulating themselves on their escape. Mouse scurried back to his burrow before the doves had a chance to thank him for their rescue.

Crow stared down in amazement. He had wanted to help the doves but had not known how. But Mouse had known just what to do, and he had the right equipment to do it with—his teeth.

Mouse was about to enter his hole when he noticed Crow for the first time. Crow was leaning over on his branch with his beak wide open. "Please, Mr. Mouse," he said, "I would like to be your friend."

I don't know who was more surprised by these words—Crow or Mouse—because the crow had always been the mouse's enemy, and so of course no mouse had even been the friend of a crow.

Although this was true, Mouse somehow knew that Crow was serious—and also sincere. Crow said next, "I watched the doves as they got caught and then escaped, and then I saw you set them free." Crow stopped and thought. He just couldn't think how to say all that was on his mind.

"I'll be your friend, if you like," Mouse said, before disappearing down his hole. He was anxious to take a nap after all the hard work he had done.

From that day on, Mouse and Crow shared their stories and experiences, and called on each other for favors and advice.

Although Crow was happy because of his friendship with Mouse, he was not pleased with his new home in the meadow. One day he asked Mouse if they could move away and start a new life by a pond, where his friend Tortoise lived.

After thinking it over, Mouse agreed. He swept out his burrow for the last time and after gathering his few belongings, he climbed up on Crow's back and they flew off together.

This time Crow made his home in a willow tree high above the water, while Mouse built a new, private burrow near the bank. Tortoise looked on from her rock at the edge of the pond. She was pleased with the new friend she had made and with the return of her old friend, Crow.

Crow and Mouse were hardly settled into their new quarters, however, when—to everybody's surprise—a long-legged, white gazelle came bounding into their lair from out of a neighboring wood. Crow flew straight up into his tree, Tortoise slid off her rock into the pond, and Mouse jumped down into his burrow.

When they had collected their wits and looked out from their secret hiding places, the three friends saw the gazelle quietly drinking from the pond.

Crow puffed up his feathers, stuck out his chest, lowered his voice, and said with authority, "What is the matter, Miss Gazelle?"

"I've been fleeing hunters," Miss Gazelle replied, looking up and panting. "I lost them in the woods. Just as soon as I get a drink from your pond, I'll be bounding off again."

The three friends gathered around Gazelle to assure her that if she were to stay with them and be their friend, she would be safe from all hunters. "We are a team," Crow explained.

"That's right," Mouse said. Tortoise poked her head in and out of her shell in agreement, which action, she felt, spoke louder than words.

Gazelle decided to stay, and to her surprise she soon became fond of her three new friends.

Mouse and Crow and Tortoise were homebodies, but Gazelle liked to wander in the surrounding woods and explore hidden places. Sometimes she would be gone all day and most of the night, but every evening she returned to share her adventures and new experiences with her friends.

Many seasons passed in this way until one unhappy day Gazelle did not return to their camp in the evening. Mouse and Crow and Tortoise were very worried. "What should we do?" they kept repeating to one another. "What should we do?"

That night they didn't try to sleep but stayed up all night trying to figure out what to do. Early the next morning Crow flew off over the woods and across the meadow. It wasn't long before he spotted Gazelle trapped in a net!

Crow swooped down beside Gazelle. "Don't worry," he said, "please don't worry. I'm sure we'll find a way to save you." Although Crow had seen a hunter approaching, he knew that if he could bring Mouse to rescue Gazelle before the hunter arrived, his friend would be saved.

Crow flew back at once and told Mouse and Tortoise what he had seen. He lifted Mouse up with his strong legs, and they flew off to rescue Gazelle. Tortoise scurried after them as fast as her short legs allowed.

Gazelle looked pitiful, all scrunched up in the net, but when she saw her friends she smiled feebly.

Mouse chewed away at the snare while Crow stood guard. But in the excitement, Crow forgot all about the approaching hunter. By the time Mouse had freed Gazelle, Tortoise had showed up, and when she saw Gazelle being freed she gave out a loud cheer. Just as she did, the four friends heard the hammer of a gun going back into position, and they turned to see the hunter taking careful aim at Gazelle.

Before he could fire, Gazelle leaped into the woods and raced away. Crow flew straight up into the air, and Mouse scurried into the underbrush. But Tortoise had nowhere to hide.

The hunter grabbed Tortoise and made a noose around her shell. Then he tossed Tortoise over his shoulder and headed off through the woods in pursuit of Gazelle.

Gazelle made a wide circle and returned to her friends, who quickly told her what had happened to Tortoise. The three friends put their heads together and devised a clever plan to rescue Tortoise.

That night Gazelle circled ahead of the hunter and lay down in his path, pretending to be wounded. This was Crow's signal to fly down and begin pecking at Gazelle's imaginary wound.

When the hunter saw Gazelle lying down, he lurched forward and pulled out his knife, and as he did, Tortoise slipped free from his shoulder. Before the hunter could reach her, Gazelle slowly rose to her feet and hobbled off through the trees, still pretending to be wounded. She led the hunter on a wild chase through the woods. Crow and Mouse flew back to Tortoise, and Mouse began chewing the noose around Tortoise's shell.

By the time the hunter gave up the chase and returned for Tortoise, the friends had safely escaped. Crow, Mouse, and Tortoise hurried home through the woods, knowing that Gazelle would be waiting for them at the pond.

Discouraged by his bad luck, and sensing an omen, the hunter moved away to another land, far, far away. Gazelle, Mouse, Tortoise, and wise old Crow embraced each other and rejoiced, knowing they would be able to live with each other in happiness and peace forever.

Kalilah wa Dimna (*Bidpai*)

The Camel and the Mouse

One day an untended camel was approached by a mouse. "Let me lead you," the mouse said. Since the camel had nowhere to go and no one to protect him, he agreed to follow the mouse.

Taking the camel's halter in his hand, the mouse began to march the camel across the wilderness. It wasn't long before they came to a swift and angry river. The mouse pulled back from the shore, but the camel stepped into the water. It was up to his knees.

"Take me up on your shoulders and carry me across the river," the mouse commanded, "or I will drown."

"You should have thought of this before you tried to become a leader," the camel answered, and marched across the river by himself.

Rumi

26/ HERON WOOS CRANE

Heron Woos Crane

Crane and Heron lived at opposite ends of a very large marsh. One day Heron said to himself, while thinking out loud, "It is about time I got married." This was obviously something he had given some thought to because once the words were out of his mouth, it was as if his mind had been made up.

Now you would have thought he would go in search of a female heron, but that is not what he did. Instead, he said to himself, "Why don't I go wading across the marsh and woo Miss Crane."

And that was what he did. When he reached Miss Crane's house at last, he called to her to see if she was at home.

"I am here," Crane called down, "what do you want?"

"Why, I want to marry you," Heron said. "I want you to be my wife."

"What an outrageous idea!" Crane said to Heron. "I won't even consider it. Your vest is short, your legs are long, and your flight is wobbly and weak. When you add all that up it means that you'll never be able to provide for me."

So back the heron marched on his spindly legs through seven miles of marsh.

But he was hardly out of Crane's sight when she began to think over his proposal. "Hmmmm," she murmured to herself, "haven't I been a spinster long enough? Shouldn't I get married? Well, *shouldn't I?*" she reasoned with herself.

So she followed Heron across the marsh and called up to his humble seat, perched atop its wobbly stick foundation. "Mr. Heron," she called up. "Oh, Mr. Heron," she intoned, ever so sweetly. "Were you serious when you said you wanted to marry me?"

"No, I was not," Heron shouted down from his perch. He was still offended by Crane's rejection, and he was in no mood to listen to her just then. This, at least, is what he told himself; but the truth was he had simply changed his mind. Crane continued to stand there, without speaking or moving. Heron looked down at her at last and said, "Why, I wouldn't marry you for all the fish in this marsh. Go away, you long-legged old maid."

The crane was so ashamed that she began sobbing. She slowly turned around and walked all the way back across the long marsh, with her head hanging very, very low.

But this time it was the heron who had second thoughts. "I shouldn't have been so peevish," he muttered to himself, while sitting on his nest looking out over the water. "I really don't like nesting alone. Perhaps I should go back and propose once again."

When Heron reached Crane's home, he called up to her, "Miss Crane, oh Miss Crane, I've changed my mind, Miss Crane. I would like to marry you after all."

This time it was Crane's turn to be peevish. "I've also changed my mind," she called back. "I wouldn't marry you for anything. Not *anything* in the whole wide world."

Once more, Heron trudged back home. But would you believe it, he was hardly out of Crane's sight when she changed her mind *again*. "Oh, I've been a fool," she squeaked. "I don't want to live alone. It's settled. Yes, it's settled. I'll marry Mr. Heron."

A long time has passed, but nothing has changed. The crane and the heron are still going back and forth across the marsh, wooing each other and then changing their minds. To this day, one of them wants to get married, and the other does not.

Russian

Anansi Rides Tiger

One day when Anansi and the Lion King were chatting in the Holy Grove of the Imperial Jungle, Anansi boasted that he liked to ride Tiger.

The King did not believe Anansi, who was, after all, a mere spider, although, the King had to admit, a very clever spider indeed. Instead of calling Anansi a liar to his face, as he might have done, he asked Tiger himself if it were true that Anansi sometimes rode on his back.

Tiger was outraged and let out a mighty roar, which not only said, "No!" but was meant to let the mighty Lion King know that he, the noble Tiger, was offended by Anansi's lie. After he had calmed down he set off in search of Anansi, to make him take back his words to the King.

When Anansi saw Tiger coming, stalking angrily through the canebrake, he pretended to be ill. But Tiger insisted that they go before the King so Anansi could confess that he had lied.

"Oh, but I can't travel now," Anansi pleaded. "I am much too ill."

"I will not take 'no' for an answer," Tiger replied. "I have been insulted before the King, my name has been tarnished, my reputation ruined."

"But friend Tiger, I can't walk," Anansi said. "I can't even stand."

"You will appear before the King if I have to carry you there myself!"

"I suppose so, then," Anansi said, "if you were to carry me on your back. Still . . . I am so weak that I would surely fall off if I didn't have a saddle to brace my feet."

Without another word Tiger dashed off and returned with a saddle.

"Now you will appear before the King."

"I suppose so," Anansi said. "Perhaps I could make it to the Imperial Jungle, if I had a bridle to hold on to."

Tiger grunted and ran off. He soon returned with a bridle.

"Yes, perhaps I could get there," Anansi said, "but only if I have a whip to swish away the flies."

Once again Tiger ran off and returned with a whip. "No more excuses," he said and picked Anansi up with his paw and flipped him onto his back. "Now we will go before the King and you can tell him that you lied."

Anansi showed no signs of illness when Tiger came galloping before the King. He was standing up in the saddle, pulling on the bridle and plying the whip to Tiger's shanks. "Come and see," he shouted to the King of the jungle, "Anansi rides Tiger!"

West African

Pig and Bear

There once was a pig and a bear who decided to go into business. They each rented a booth at the local bazaar. Pig roasted a heap of potatoes, and Bear fried up a batch of donuts.

They got to the marketplace ahead of everyone else and set up their booths. It was a crisp, clear day and perfect, they both thought, for selling steaming potatoes and fresh, warm donuts.

Bear had a nickel in his vest. Before the first customer arrived he went over to Pig's stall. "How much are you getting for one of those potatoes?" he asked.

"A nickel." Pig said.

Bear had wanted to say that he was just curious about the price, and that he had come over to make conversation. But instead, he fished the nickel out of his pocket, laid it down on the counter, and picked up a steaming hot potato with one of his paws. He crossed back over to his own counter and began eating his potato.

Business is thriving, Pig thought. But since no one was waiting in line, he walked over to Bear's stand and purchased a strawberry-filled donut for a nickel.

Bear was pleased to have made a sale. Before another customer showed up he thought he might have something more to eat. He crossed over to Pig's stand and bought another potato.

Bear considered this a lucky move, because the next thing he knew Pig was over for another donut.

There wasn't any other business at the moment, until Bear bought another potato. Then Pig came over and bought a donut. Bear came back for another potato.

This happened several times more, back and forth, with Pig's and Bear's stomachs growing noticeably larger.

It wasn't long before every single potato and every last donut were sold and eaten.

"What do you think?" Bear said to Pig. "I suppose we ought to count our money." When they did they found that Bear had a nickel and Pig had nothing.

They couldn't believe their eyes.

"But we both sold out," Pig declared, "and we have no money!"

Bear looked down at his nickel and scratched his head. It wasn't until he had walked all the way back home that he realized it was the same nickel he had started with.

Czechoslovakian

Doctor Toad

A toad hung a mortar and pestle around his neck, and taking a jar of ointment in his hand, he began wandering the countryside.

Wherever he went, he announced, "I am the doctor. I know the cure for every illness!"

All the animals flocked around him to be healed of their afflictions. But when the fox came by and had a good look at the doctor, he said, "What nonsense! *You* are nothing but humps and bumps from head to foot, and yet you claim that you can cure others."

Armenian

The Peacock and the Jackdaw

The birds of a certain territory were arguing over who should be chosen as their king. The peacock strutted forth into the center of the conference and spread his beautiful tail, stating that he alone was worthy of the honor, since no other could surpass his beauty. The birds were about to select him as their king, when the jackdaw spoke up. "What good would your fine feathers be, oh peacock," he asked, "if we were attacked and our survival depended on your beauty?"

Aesop

Coyote and the Acorns

One day Coyote was visiting his relatives and was given sour acorns to eat. He had never eaten anything quite so delicious in all his life. "How were these prepared?" he asked. "You must have a secret recipe."

"No secret at all," they answered. "You put them in water, press them down hard, and in two days' time they are ready to eat."

That's too easy, Coyote thought, they're putting me on. "That can't be the only way," he said. "There must be another way, or else something you're not telling me."

They insisted that sour acorns were prepared in just that manner, but Coyote did not believe them and kept insisting there must be a secret that they were hiding from him.

They soon became exasperated and said, "All right, this is how it is done. You load a canoe with acorns, tip it over and drown them. Then when they float back up and begin to be carried downstream, you walk along the riverbank and pick them up."

Coyote was delighted. He had obtained the secret at last. He ran home at once to tell his grandmother. "What kind of recipe is that!" she exclaimed. "If you want sour acorns you have to dampen them first and then press them."

"Not at all," Coyote said. "You drown them."

Before she could utter another word, Coyote snatched up all her acorns and dumped them in the river. But when he walked along the bank he couldn't find a single acorn, because all of the acorns had drowned.

Yurok Indian, Southwestern United States

The Ungrateful Wolf
and the Gullible Heron

One day a wolf got a bone stuck in his throat. He approached a heron and promised her a reward if she would stretch her long neck down inside his throat and pull the bone free.

But when the bone had been removed and the heron asked for her fee, the cunning wolf said, "You have already been paid. I had you in my throat and I let you go free."

Babrius

The Monkey and the Crocodile

Once upon a time a monkey was visited by a crocodile. This is how it happened.

Monkey lived in one of the tallest trees on a riverbank where there were many crocodiles. One of these crocodiles had been watching Monkey for a very long time. She had a son who was very difficult to train because he was stupid. One day she called him to her side and said, "My son, I want the heart of a monkey to eat. See that monkey in yonder tree? I want you to go fetch his heart."

"How can I do that?" the young crocodile answered. "I do not travel on land and monkeys don't go in the water."

"Use your crocodile wits," his mother said. "That's what they are for."

Crocodile took himself to a log and floated past Monkey's home, while he thought and thought.

Finally it occurred to him that he might be able to entice Monkey to go across the river to one of the islands where the fruit had become ripe.

Crocodile slid off his log and swam under Monkey's tree. "Monkey, Monkey," he called up, "how would you like to go to an island where the fruit is ripe?"

"But how can I do that," Monkey shouted down at Crocodile, "when I cannot swim?"

"I already thought of that," Crocodile said. "You can travel on my back."

Well, Monkey was as greedy as Crocodile was stupid. Without thinking, he swung down from his tree and landed on Crocodile's back.

"Here we go," Crocodile said, "hold on tight."

"I'm enjoying the ride," Monkey said.

"Is that right?" Crocodile said. "Well, how do you like this!" and down dove Crocodile to the bottom of the river.

When they came back up Monkey was coughing and choking so hard he could hardly speak. "Why did you do that?" he asked Crocodile. "I nearly drowned."

"That's the idea," Crocodile said. "I'm going to take your heart to my mother because she wants a monkey's heart to eat."

"Well, why didn't you say so," Monkey replied. "If I had known that, I would have brought my heart along."

"Do you mean to tell me," Crocodile sputtered, "that you left your heart back in that tree?"

"That's right," Monkey said. "If you want my heart you'll have to take me back. But first can't we go to the island for some fruit?"

"Nothing doing," Crocodile said. "First your heart, then the fruit."

But no sooner was Monkey safely back on land than he scampered up his tree and began taunting Crocodile. "Here I am, you stupid crocodile. My heart is here, and my heart is in me. If you can fly as well as you can swim, you are welcome to come up here and take us both to your mother."

Indian

The Lemming and the Owl

An owl saw a lemming feeding just outside its hole. He flew down and said to the lemming, "Two dog teams are heading in this direction!"

But the lemming understood the owl's game. Peering up at him from under a bush, she said, "You can have me to eat, if you like, Owl. It is much better to be consumed by one's neighbor than by strangers one has never seen before. As you can see, I am quite plump and will make a good meal. Indeed, if you would like to celebrate before you eat me, I will be happy to sing while you dance."

The owl was overjoyed. He puffed himself up and began to dance to the lemming's tune. Looking up at the sky while he danced, he forgot all about the lemming. As the owl hopped from side to side, the lemming saw her chance and dashed between the owl's legs and raced down her hole.

The owl called down to the lemming to come out, saying the dog teams had passed. But the wise lemming was safe now, and backing up in her hole, she kicked dirt in the owl's face.

Eskimo

52/THE WOLF AND THE SEVEN LITTLE KIDS

The Wolf
and the Seven Little Kids

There once was a nanny goat with seven little kids. One day, when she was about to go into the woods for her daily search for food, she gathered her kids together and warned them about a wolf that lived in the neighborhood.

"Beware of the wolf while I am away," she said to them. "Should he ever get into the house he will eat each of you whole—hair, skin, teeth, and tail. The wolf is very clever and is an expert at disguise. But you will know him by his rough voice and black paws."

The kids assured their mother they would be safe, but she was barely out of sight when they heard a knocking at the door.

"Open up, my dear little children, it is your mother with something good to eat," the wolf commanded.

"We will not, we will not," chorused the kids. "Our mother's voice is gentle and yours is rough, and this must mean that you are the wolf."

The wolf went to a neighboring shop and bought a stick of chalk, which he ate to make his voice soft. He returned to Nanny Goat's house and knocked again on the door.

"Open the door for your mother, children, I've brought you something good to eat."

None of the kids could tell for sure if it was their mother's voice they were hearing, but one of them kneeled down and saw a black foot under the door. He stood up and shouted, "We won't open the door. Your foot is black and our mother's is not, and that must mean that you are the wolf."

The wolf ran off to the baker and said, "I have banged my back paws on a rock. Please put some dough on them so they will heal."

Then the wolf raced off to the miller. "Please spread some flour on my back paws," he pleaded.

But the miller knew the wolf's game and refused.

"First I said 'please,'" the wolf roared, "and now I say *you'd better*, or I'll eat you up—flour, apron, cap, and all."

The miller immediately whitened the wolf's paws.

The wolf returned to Nanny Goat's house and knocked for the third time on her door.

"Open up, children, your mother has brought each of you a present from the woods."

"First show us your feet, so we will know if you are our mother, or the wolf."

The wolf pushed his two back feet under the door.

When they saw that his paws were white they believed he was their mother, and they opened the door.

The wolf charged into the house and began chasing the squealing goats. The kids ran helter-skelter, each in a different direction. One jumped into bed, another under the table, a third into the oven, the fourth into a kitchen cupboard, a fifth into a bin of potatoes, a sixth into the washtub, and the seventh hid in the tall clock case.

The wolf found all but one and swallowed them whole, just as their mother had warned them he would do. But the wolf could not find the kid in the clock case.

Even so he was so stuffed by the time he ate the sixth kid, that he was barely able to get through the kitchen door. He got as far as the meadow below the house, where he soon fell asleep under a tree.

The kitchen door was standing open when Nanny Goat returned. And, oh, what a sight: chairs here, tables there, crocks broken, benches and basins overturned, covers and pillows torn. She searched everywhere but not a kid could she find. She called each of their names, over and over again, but no one answered. And then, just when she had given up hope, a tiny voice squeaked, "Here mother, I am over here in the clock case." It was the voice of the youngest kid, the only one that had survived.

When he was safely out of the case, he told his mother what had happened. She wept and wept over the loss of her six little children. In a daze she wandered down to the meadow with her smallest kid following behind. It wasn't long before they spotted the wolf sleeping under a tree.

They crept up and peered at his stomach. It was moving from side to side!

Nanny Goat whispered to her youngest, "Hurry! Run home and bring me back scissors, needle, and thread."

When he returned, she quickly cut a hole in the wolf's side, and out popped the head of one of her kids. It wasn't long before all six of her children had leaped out of the gaping hole.

After they had frolicked and danced about awhile, Nanny Goat said, "Hurry, run down to the river and bring me some stones."

She stuffed the wolf with the stones they brought and sewed up his stomach as fast as she could.

When the wolf woke up he felt very thirsty, but when he started for the river the stones began to rattle and roll inside him. "What's this tumbling in my stomach? I thought it was six kids I ate, not a sack of rolling stones."

Bending over the bank for a drink the wolf fell down from the weight of the stones and was dragged to the bottom of the river, where he quickly drowned.

Nanny Goat and her kids stared down into the water and hugged each other tight.

The wolf lay dead, at the bottom of the river, and for all anyone knows he may be there still.

Brothers Grimm

Caucasian Riddle

There once lived an elephant who was presented with a riddle by his father. He was given a goat, a wolf, and a cabbage that he had to carry from the island they were on to their mainland home. He was given one rule: he could carry only one of them across the river at a time.

Now the elephant knew that if he left the goat, the wolf, and the cabbage alone together, the goat would eat the cabbage, and the wolf would eat the goat. How then was the elephant going to get himself and all three—goat, wolf, and cabbage—safely onto the mainland?

There was a solution to the riddle, of course, otherwise it wouldn't have been a riddle, and it took the elephant a very long time to figure out that to solve his problem he would have to make one extra trip.

Gurdjieff

The Incautious Fox
and the Foolish Wolf

One moonlit evening a fox was passing by a well in the forest of a foolish wolf. The fox looked down the well and mistook the moon reflected in the water for a round of cheese.

Leaning on one of the buckets used for raising water, he lost his balance and went crashing to the bottom of the well. The other bucket, which had been in the well, went flying up, as the bucket that held the fox went down, down, down into the water.

"So that's what the bucket was for," the fox said under his breath. "I could have had real water to drink instead of imaginary cheese."

Time went by, and with it the paring of the moon. "There is no time to waste," thought the fox still in the bottom of the well. "I will be dead soon if someone does not come along and mistake the reflection of the slowly diminishing moon for an appetizing round of cheese as I did."

Just then the foolish wolf came strolling by, famished as usual. "I have a treat for you," the wolf heard a voice cry out from inside the well. "Come and see for yourself."

The wolf peered down into the well. The voice said, "Only a sliver has been eaten, the rest is for you. Come down in the bucket that is dangling over the well."

The wolf jumped into the bucket at the top of the well and came hurling down, while the fox in his bucket flew straight up out of the well and went racing back to the land from which he had come.

La Fontaine

Monkey

In a time long, long ago, there existed a rock that was as old as creation. It was made of the pure essences of Heaven, and it was as fruitful as the Earth that bore it. One day it split open and gave birth to a stone egg the size of a ball, and in this egg was a monkey, complete in every organ and limb.

Although it could climb and run and do all the things that monkeys do, from the moment it was born its first act was to bow towards each of the Four Quarters, and flashing its steely eyes, it cast a light as far as the Palace of the Pole Star.

The Jade Emperor, sitting in the Cloud Mists and surrounded by his Fairy Ministers, was astonished. Watching this strange light as it continued to flash, he ordered Thousand-league Eye and Down-the-wind Ears to open the gate of the Southern Heaven and to look out.

The ministers soon returned and gave their report, saying that the steely light was coming from the borders of the small country of Ao-lai, from the Mountain of Flowers and Fruit.

Further, they told the Jade Emperor that on this mountain there existed a magic rock, which had given birth to a monkey, and when he bowed to the Four Quarters a steely light flashed from his eyes with a beam that reached the Palace of the Pole Star.

The Jade Emperor thought a moment and then said, "These creatures in the world below were compounded of the essence of Heaven and Earth, and nothing that goes on down there should surprise us."

Meanwhile, Monkey cavorted to his heart's content, drinking freely from the rivers and springs and gathering mountain flowers and the fruits of the seasons. He made friends of all the animals. For companions he had Panther, Tiger, and Wolf, and his other friends included the deer and civet cats, not to mention gibbons and baboons, who were his kindred.

Monkey wandered among the caves and mountain peaks by day, and at night he slept under protective cliffs.

One morning Monkey went to bathe in a mountain stream in the company of other monkeys. One of the monkeys said, "None of us knows where this stream comes from. I think it would be fun to follow it to its source." The words were hardly out of his mouth when all the other monkeys began screaming with joy. Carrying their children and calling out to their other kin, they rushed along the stream and scrambled up the side of a bordering cliff, until at last they found themselves standing before the curtain of a great waterfall. Clapping their hands and jumping up and down, they sang out, "Lovely water! Oh, lovely water!"

One of the monkeys shouted above the roar, "Just think, this water starts off in some cavern far below the base of the mountain, and from there it flows away to the Great Sea!"

Another monkey said, "We would make that one our king who could boldly pierce that water curtain, find the source of that stream, and then return to us unharmed."

Three times this challenge was made before Monkey leaped out of the throng. "I will go!" he cried out. "I will go and see what is there."

Monkey screwed up his eyes and crouched down. Then, with a single leap, he bounced straight through the waterfall. When Monkey opened his eyes and looked around him, he saw that he had landed on a spot where there was no water. Instead, he was standing before a shining bridge that stretched out in front of him, glistening into the distance. On close examination he saw that it was made of burnished iron, while the water that flowed beneath it came gushing through a hole in a rock, filling the space formed by the arch.

Monkey climbed up on the bridge, and gazing left and right as he walked along, he noticed an object that looked like a house. There below him were stone seats and stone couches, and tables with stone bowls and cups. He hurried back to the entrance of the bridge, where he saw inscribed on the cliff in large square letters the following statement: *This cave of the Water Curtain, in the blessed land of the Mountain of Flowers and Fruit and the Heavenly Grotto of the Water Curtain Cave, leads to Heaven.*

Monkey was beside himself. He rushed back to the spot where he had entered, and again crouching, he shut his eyes and jumped back through the curtain of water.

The other monkeys surrounded him at once. "What a great stroke of luck!" Monkey cried out. "What a great stroke of luck!"

"Tell us what you saw on the other side," the monkeys clamored. "Is the water very deep?"

"There *is* no water where I landed," Monkey said. "I came down beside an iron bridge that leads to a place that is pure heaven."

"What do you mean?" they screeched.

"I will tell you what I saw there," Monkey answered. "Water flows out of a hole in the rock, filling in the space underneath the bridge. At the side of the bridge are flowers and trees, where there is a chamber of stone. Inside this chamber are stone tables, stone cups, stone dishes, stone couches, and stone seats. It would be a very comfortable place for us to live. There is room enough for hundreds and thousands of us, both the young and the old. I think we should go there and live because we will be sheltered in all kinds of weather."

The monkeys jumped up and down and began shouting, "You go first, you go first, and show us how."

Once again Monkey closed his eyes and bounded through the curtain of water. From the other side he cried out, "Come along, all of you!"

The boldest monkeys jumped through at once, but the more timid ones stretched their heads halfway through the curtain and then drew their heads back, scratching their ears and rubbing their cheeks. This went on for some time before all of them—as if held by an invisible string—leaped through in a single body.

It wasn't any time at all before they began grabbing bowls and cups, fighting for the beds, and dragging things around and shifting them about, behaving for all the world just the way mischievous monkeys always behave: screeching, and never quiet for an instant. Until, at last, they dropped from exhaustion.

Monkey took his seat at the head of them and said, "Fellow monkeys! If your words are not to be trusted, then what is the use! You promised that the one who was able to get through the waterfall and come back again would be your king. I have gone through the curtain not once, but twice, and not only that, I have found you a comfortable place to sleep, and I have put you in the enviable position of being householders. Therefore, why do you not bow down to me as your king?"

The monkeys needed only to be reminded. They drew up in a line, according to age and standing, and bowing humbly with their palms pressed together, they cried out, "Great King, a thousand years!"

From that time on, the stone monkey discarded his old name and took the title Handsome Monkey King. He appointed various monkeys, gibbons, and baboons to be his ministers and officers. By day they wandered about the Mountain of Flowers and Fruit, and at night they slept in the Grotto of the Water Curtain.

They lived in perfect sympathy and accord, independent of all the other beasts, and were happy and content. And thus it remained for hundreds and hundreds of years.

Chinese (from Journey to the West,
by Wu Cheng-en)

Armenian Proverb

Pigs never see the stars.

African Proverb

Even the greatest bird must descend from the sky
to find a tree to roost upon.

76/THE HERON AND THE HUMMINGBIRD

The Heron
and the Hummingbird

Heron and Hummingbird lived together on the shores of the Atlantic Ocean. One day Hummingbird challenged Heron to a race.

"I can't race you," Heron said. "I almost never fly, and you seem never to sit. You are so swift and agile, and I am so slow and clumsy."

But Hummingbird kept after Heron to race, until one day Heron agreed.

They decided to race from the Atlantic Ocean in the East to the Pacific Ocean in the West.

They drew a line at the water's edge and began their race.

Heron had barely lifted his wings and tucked up his feet, when Hummingbird was out of sight. But Heron kept flapping and flying, and it wasn't long before he began to glide along with a slow and steady motion.

At nightfall, Hummingbird flew to a tree and stopped for the night, while Heron continued his flight. But it wasn't until daybreak that he reached the tree where Hummingbird was sleeping.

The sun had not even reached mid-sky before Hummingbird had already passed Heron on the following day.

That night Hummingbird rested again, but this time she was passed by Heron, before midnight.

The next day Hummingbird didn't pass Heron until noon.

On the third night Heron caught up with Hummingbird well before midnight, and Hummingbird did not pass Heron on the following day until late afternoon.

Once more Hummingbird rested at nightfall, and again she was passed by Heron, who still hadn't slept but had flown with a slow but steady rhythm toward his destination. The next morning Heron arrived at the Pacific Ocean far ahead of Hummingbird, who was surprised to learn, when she finally arrived at the ocean's edge, that she had lost the race.

Muskogee Indian, Southeastern United States

The Blue Jackal

Far away, in a damp and lonely cave, lived a jackal named Fierce-Howl, who could be seen from time to time in the city streets searching for food. He only ventured into the city when he was desperate, for the loud, barking dogs of the city streets were his natural enemies.

Now it happened late one evening that he was trapped in an alley by a gang of dogs. It was only because of his great speed that he was able to escape. After a long, frightening run, the jackal spotted an open door that he did not know led into the shop of a dyer. To hide from the dogs he jumped into a vat of indigo.

The dogs searched everywhere before giving up and wandering back to the streets. Thoroughly soaked and feeling downright miserable, the jackal crawled out of the vat and fled into the forest. The following day all of the animals of that region began talking about the creature with the glistening blue coat. They never suspected that this shiny new creature was the tired old hungry jackal that lived alone in a cave. "Oh my," they said to one another. "Oh dear, oh dear, oh dear, it must be a bad omen. Yes, yes, it must certainly be." And one by one they began to pack their belongings in readiness to leave this place where the blue creature lived.

When Fierce-Howl realized the effect he was having, he called out, "Do not be afraid, you creatures of the wild, the gods of the forest have appointed me your leader. I am called King Fierce-Howl. You may all live here in safety within the boundaries I have formed with my unconquerable paws."

When the animals heard this they marched forward and, bowing humbly, said, "Master, tell us our duties."

Fierce-Howl appointed the lion prime minister; the tiger, lord of the bedchamber; the leopard, master of the kitchen; and the elephant, doorkeeper. The monkey became the bearer of the royal parasol. But he boxed the ears of his own kind, the jackals, and drove them away.

In this fashion, Fierce-Howl enjoyed all the glories and privileges of a king.

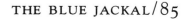

Time passed.

One day, while sitting in his court, he heard the howling of a pack of jackals nearby. It had been so long since he had heard the voices of his own kind, that a shiver of satisfaction ran up his spine, while his eyes filled with tears of joy. He leaped up, and with his eyes closed, he began howling, with his snout facing the direction of the other voices.

All at once the other animals realized that King Fierce-Howl was nothing more than a jackal in disguise. "We have been deceived," they shouted. "We have been deceived. King Fierce-Howl is only a jackal. He surely must die."

Fierce-Howl tried to run for his life, but he was caught by a tiger who quickly tore him to pieces. And so ended the short, happy reign of Fierce-Howl, who achieved his authority by accident and a trick, and lost it just as easily by accident and a slip.

The Panchatantra

The Oh So Grand Ox, and the Poor Pathetic Frog

One day an ox, having wandered far from his home, came to a pond that was filled with water lilies. He did not notice the croaking frog who was trying very hard to get his attention. Although the ox heard the croaking, he had no idea what it meant, or even who was doing it. He was too busy admiring the water lilies.

Meanwhile, the frog—who had never before seen a creature so large or majestic, so proud or mysterious, or so strange—found herself growing larger and larger in an attempt to be noticed. Croaking and puffing, and puffing and croaking, she sprang from her lily pad to the shore, but she still couldn't get the ox's attention.

Finally, the frog began rolling on her sides, and twisting her head this way and that, to see if she had been noticed, until her outer skin was so completely filled with hot air that she exploded.

The ox looked down to see what had made such a noise, but the frog of course was no longer there.

La Fontaine

THE OH SO GRAND OX, AND THE POOR PATHETIC FROG/89

The Stolen Moon

No one knew how Bear had come to possess the moon. All the other animals knew was that the moon—the round, familiar moon—was no longer in the sky. There were many who wanted the moonlight, but they could not persuade Bear to give up the moon. They did not know that Bear had tied up the moon in a bag and hidden it under his bed. They only knew that Bear preferred the darkness.

Fox wanted the moon. He wanted the moon to make moonlight, so he could hunt by its light. He went to Raven, who was Bear's uncle, and asked for his help. Raven also wanted moonlight, and so together they made a plan and hurried off to Bear's camp.

Bear made them welcome, and after they were comfortably seated, Raven began telling stories. This was part of their secret plan. It wasn't long before Bear grew drowsy. Raven told one monotonous story after another, and Bear grew more and more sleepy. But every time he nodded off, he quickly awoke with a start, for something told him he must not fall asleep.

While Raven was telling stories, Fox was peering around the room in search of the hidden moon. Just as Bear was nodding off for the very last time, Fox spotted the tied-up bag under Bear's bed. It was evening and the glow of the moon had begun to light up the cloth pouch. Fox ran and grabbed the bag by its strings, carried it outdoors, and hurled the moon into the sky.

Bear came awake at that very moment, and pushing open the window, he cried, "Come back, moon, come back. I don't want you to shine."

But Fox shouted even louder, "Fly away, moon, fly away, and give us your light."

Some say they were both successful, while others say they both failed. For some evenings are filled with moonlight, and on other evenings there is no moon at all.

Kutchin Indian, Canada

Sources

Aesop was believed to have been a Phrygian slave who lived in the sixth century B.C. The first printed edition of Aesop's fables in English appeared in 1484. Many similarities have been found between his fables and those of the *Panchatantra.*

Babrius was a hellenized Italian who was born at the end of the first century A.D. He was the first translator to put Aesopic fables into iambic verse.

The Fables of Bidpai were originally written in Sanskrit and were attributed to an Indian sage named Bidpai (or Pilpay) as instructions for the behavior of the young princes of the Indian court. They were then carried to Persia and translated into Pehlevi.

Jean de la Fontaine was born in 1621 to an upper-class French family. He first published his witty *Contes* and *Fables* between 1664 and 1668.

The Brothes Grimm (Jacob, born in 1785, and Wilhelm, born in 1786, in Germany) collaborated and faithfully recorded the disappearing folklore of their people.

G. I. Gurdjieff (1877–1949) was born in Alexandropol of a Greek father and an Armenian mother. In 1922 he founded *The Institute for the Harmonious Development of Man* near Fontainebleu in France.

Jalal-uddin Rumi (1207–1273) was a mystic and poet whose *Mathnawi,* from which the tale herein was taken, is a classic of Sufism. Rumi was also the founder of the Sufi order called the Mevlevi dervishes, known for their whirling dances of ecstacy.

Kalilah wa Dimna—as the Fables of Bidpai were called in Persia—became popular throughout the Near and Middle East.

Panchatantra (the name means five books, or Pentateuch) was said to have been written in India earlier than 200 B.C. as a guide to wisdom for conducting one's life.

Wu Cheng-en lived during the sixteenth century A.D. His most famous work, *Monkey (Journey to the West)*, is a brilliant combination of allegory, religion, satire, and poetry, and is the most famous and widely read novel in the history of Chinese literature.

The End